PETER'S CHAIR

EZRA JACK KEATS

PETER'S CHAIR

Harper & Row, Publishers · New York, Evanston, and London

For Joan Roseman

Peter stretched as high as he could.
There! His tall building was finished.

CRASH! Down it came.
"Shhhh!" called his mother.
"You'll have to play more quietly.
Remember, we have a new baby in the house."

Peter looked into his sister Susie's room.
His mother was fussing around the cradle.
"That's my cradle," he thought,
"and they painted it pink!"

"Hi, Peter," said his father.
"Would you like to help paint sister's high chair?"
"It's my high chair," whispered Peter.

He saw his crib and muttered,
"My crib. It's painted pink too."
Not far away stood his old chair.
"They didn't paint that yet!" Peter shouted.

He picked it up and ran to his room.

"Let's run away, Willie," he said.
Peter filled a shopping bag
with cookies and dog biscuits.
"We'll take my blue chair, my toy crocodile,
and the picture of me when I was a baby."
Willie got his bone.

They went outside and stood in front of his house.
"This is a good place," said Peter.
He arranged his things very nicely
and decided to sit in his chair for a while.

But he couldn't fit in the chair. He was too big!

His mother came to the window and called,
"Won't you come back to us, Peter dear?
We have something very special for lunch."
Peter and Willie made believe they didn't hear.
But Peter got an idea.

Soon his mother saw signs that Peter was home.
"That rascal is hiding behind the curtain,"
she said happily.

She moved the curtain away.
But he wasn't there!

"Here I am," shouted Peter.

Peter sat in a grown-up chair.
His father sat next to him.
"Daddy," said Peter, "let's paint
the little chair pink for Susie."

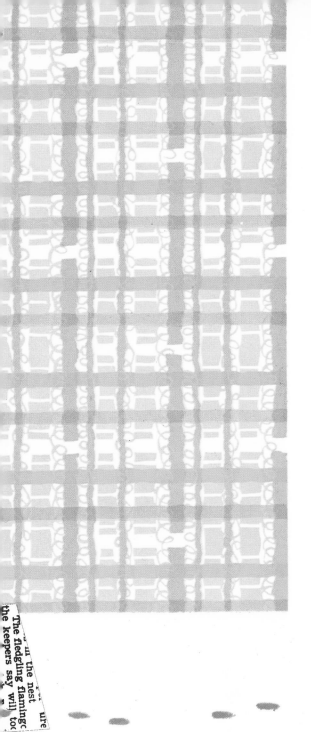

And they did.